For Bussa,
It's not *ab*

PUMPKIN BELLY

AND OTHER STORIES

Have a bellyful o fun

by
TANYA BATSON-SAVAGE

TANYA BATSON-SAVAGE '16

Illustrated by
Staysean Daley

BLUE MOON PUBLISHING KINGSTON JAMAICA.

love from Auntie Rachel &
Uncle Allan

PUMPKIN BELLY
AND OTHER STORIES

First published in Kingston by Blue Moon Publishing 2005
New edition published 2015

Cover Design Staysean Daley

PO Box 5464
Liguanea PO
Kingston 6
Jamaica, W.I.

www.blumoonbooks.com

CIP data of this book is available from the National Library of Jamaica
ISBN 978-976-95436-7-6

Printed in China

CONTENTS

To Mama Sweetie

PUMPKIN BELLY

There is something very special about Albert and it is not his yellow skin. What makes Albert special is the reason his skin is yellow. When Albert was born he had ten fingers, ten toes, two eyes, a nose, a mouth, no teeth and he was the same chocolate brown as the rest of his family. He was as normal as normal could be. Now, Albert is a bright pumpkin yellow, because that's the colour curiosity made him.

This is how it happened. One day Albert was in the kitchen with his mother. She was making soup and had a green round pumpkin. When she cut the pumpkin open Albert saw beads of water inside it. Albert stared at it in wonderment.

"Mommy! Mommy!" Albert said, tugging at his mother's skirt. "How did the water get into the pumpkin?"

"It walk," she said in that mysterious way she sometimes had. The answer did not satisfy Albert. Water couldn't walk could it? It ran, so maybe if it slowed down it could walk but where did it walk? The water was not yellow. It looked as though someone had just sprinkled some inside the pumpkin.

Filled with curiosity, Albert went over to the bankra basket on the kitchen floor. There was yam, sweet potatoes, dried coconuts, green bananas and another small pumpkin. Albert took up the pumpkin and examined its rich green skin. He looked for holes that the water could have gone through. He looked and he looked and he looked. He saw no holes. There was a small triangle cut

into the pumpkin's skin. Albert tried to pull out the triangle to see if that was where the water had walked.

"Albert, what are you doing over there?" his mother called.

"I'm trying to find where the water walked Mommy. Did it go through this triangle in the skin?"

"Don't be silly Albert," she said. "I cut that hole in the pumpkin when I bought it at the market."

Albert was confused and curious.

That night, when Albert went to bed he could think of nothing else but the mysterious water in the pumpkin. Albert wondered if water went into his own belly like that. He used to think that everything got mixed up. Did they stay separate when they were in the belly? Could you tell your fried dumplings different from your juice after you had eaten them?

Albert thought long and hard as he stared out the window. He was still thinking about this great mystery when he saw the first star of the evening. He was filled with excitement. He could simply make a wish. Albert closed his eyes and wished.

"I wish I could find out how water gets into the belly of the pumpkin," he said.

He slowly opened one eye to check if the wish had come true. Nothing had changed. Albert was disappointed. He stared out the window as the night darkened and more

stars came out. After a while, his eyes drifted close and finally he fell asleep.

Someone was poking Albert in the stomach. He moaned and rolled over. When he moved the pillow went into his mouth. It tasted funny, reminding Albert of the delicious dirt he got at his grandmother's house. Albert's eyes flew open. He looked around him in wonderment.

He was not in bed. There were giant plants all around him. Vines ran all over the ground, twisting and turning this way and that. When he looked up, he could see broad, green leaves that reached up to the sky. The sunlight came through the leaves in a greenish colour. Being in this strange place frightened Albert. He looked to his left. He looked to his right, but all he saw were leaves and vines. Then in the distance he saw see what looked like a pumpkin. A pumpkin? A giant pumpkin?

With shock and delight Albert knew where he was.

He was in a giant pumpkin patch. His wish had come true! If he was so tiny, and the pumpkin so big, maybe he could find out how the water gets into its belly. Albert trotted toward the pumpkin.

He had not gone far when he heard a sound. There was a six-legged monster coming toward him on one of the vines. It was moving at a terrible speed. Albert wanted to hide, but was fascinated by the creature. It would move and then stop, turn back the way it had come, stop again and turn around once more. When it came closer Albert saw that it was a giant ant.

"Oh no! Oh no! I can't find it! I can't find it!" the giant ant said in a high-pitched voice. "Oh peas, onions and tomatoes! Everyone else has left but I can't find it. What will I do? What will I do?" The ant spun around and around almost making Albert dizzy as he watched her. "I was walking right there, and Jane was just in front of me, and Petra was in front of her, then there was Marva, Sheila and Pam. I turned around for just one tiny teensy second and I can't find anybody. I can't find it. I can't find it! Peas, onions, toma-"

"What can't you find?" asked Albert, curiosity overcoming good sense.

"Who said that? Who said that?" asked the ant turning around in a circle.

"I did," said Albert, wondering how smart it was to

confront the giant ant. Its huge black eyes were a little scary, but the ant did not look very dangerous. Albert tugged at his belt buckle as though he was pulling at his courage.

"Maybe if you tell me what you lost I can help," he said.

"You? Help? But you don't have feelers! What are you anyway? Maybe you took it? Did you take it? Did you take it?" The ant moved toward Albert suspiciously, her little black feelers stretched out.

"It wasn't me!" cried Albert in the defence all children give when something goes missing. "Really, I didn't take it!"

The ant reached out and touched Albert with its arm like feelers. "Hmm, you don't feel like you're lying," she said. "What are you?"

"My name's Albert. What's your name?"

"Well I'm Anita. Anita Ant, a senior member in the service of her majesty queen Aretha Ant II," she replied. "But you still haven't told me what you are."

"I'm a boy," said Albert.

"You're not a boy," said Anita Ant. "Boys are nasty biggies. Always picking on us. They see us walking in a line and squash us. We don't like biggies. Always sitting in the way and never sharing their food. All they do is stomp, so that we have to scamper out of the way. I have lost many sisters to the biggies." Then she turned and looked at Albert as though she had only just remembered that he was there. "You smell like a biggie. You look like a biggie. You're just not very big."

"I might not be very big, but I am a boy," said Albert, puffing up his chest and trying to look taller.

"Are you now? We don't like boys very much," said Anita Ant and she started walking toward Albert. Now she looked scary.

"But I can help you find it!" yelped Albert in desperation.

"You can?" asked Anita Ant.

"If- if you tell me what it is," Albert finished nervously.

"Ahh biggies can't smell anything," Anita Ant said. "I'm trying to find my sisters. We were all walking in a line, like we always do, and then I just couldn't smell them any more. I'm a

complete disgrace. I've never lost a scent before. My queen will have my head."

"Don't worry. I'll help you find them, if you can tell me one thing," said Albert getting an idea.

"Okay. What do you want to know?"

"How does water get to the pumpkin's belly?"

"What? It walks. Everybody knows that! Oh just like a biggie to ask a very unimportant question at a very busy time. I've got mouths to feed, and you want to know how water gets to the belly of the pumpkin. What business of yours is it how the water gets there? I'm not searching for water. I'm hunting."

"You're hunting?" asked Albert.

"Of course," answered the ant.

"But you're a girl," said Albert. "Girls don't hunt."

"Of course we do. If the girls didn't do it who would?"

"The boys," suggested Albert.

"The boys? The boys? The boys? That's silly. Boy ants don't work! All they do is laze about in the colony," and Anita Ant began to laugh. Albert didn't see what was so funny, and he didn't like being laughed at.

Suddenly Anita Ant stopped laughing. Her feelers drummed in the air.

"There it is!" she cried. "I found it! I found it!" Then forgetting that Albert was ever there she scampered off in a great hurry.

"Wait!" Albert cried, but it was too late. The ant was gone.

Albert felt very sad about her leaving. He was so close to pumpkins and he still could not find out where the water walked. He continued to walk toward the giant pumpkin. Albert concentrated as he climbed over the pumpkin vines on the ground. Then, something he first thought was a vine moved. Albert stepped back. Before him was a lizard. Albert had not seen the lizard at first because it was almost the same shade of green as the pumpkin vines. The lizard seemed to be upset about something.

"Stupid flowers," the lizard muttered. "They think they are so cute, with the reds and yellows. I can be many colours but you don't hear me boasting about it do you? Ohh, look at me I can turn a lovely emerald green, or midnight black." As the lizard spoke of the different colours he changed into them. Albert was amazed. He had seen green lizards before but never this close. Albert inched a little closer. When he moved he stepped on a dried pumpkin leaf and it crackled under his foot. The lizard jumped around with lightning speed.

"Who is that?" he asked, turning a dark brown.

"It's me," Albert said.

"It's not me. I'm here. So it's you," the lizard replied.

"That's what I said," said Albert.

"No it's not. You said it's me. But it isn't me. It's you."

"Okay, okay," said Albert getting confused. "It's you, it's you."

"See I told you it was me," said the lizard. Then he realized that was as confused as Albert. "Oh you're tricky. Are you a spy for TFC?"

"TFC? What is that?" asked Albert.

"Oh don't pretend you don't know about them. Everybody knows about TFC – The Flowers Coalition. They will never enslave me," the lizard said looking around him as though he knew someone was watching him. "They invite you in with the promise of nectar, and when you leave pollen is stuck to you. But I'm a brilliant lizard, I graduated at the top of my tree, I know all about flowers and their tricks!"

"So do you know how water gets into the belly of the pumpkin?" Albert asked, not really thinking he would get the answer he wanted.

"Sure," said the lizard.

"How?" asked Albert trembling with excitement.

"It walks," said the lizard. Albert was crushed. Everybody told him the same thing. That was what his mother had said and now this lizard said the same thing.

"Yes, but where does it walk?" Albert asked in a small voice.

"Oh that's easy. It walks through the stem," the lizard said.

"Really?" Albert asked excitedly. He could not believe his luck. He had always thought that lizards were stupid creatures and now it was a lizard that told him what to do. "But how do I get in?" he asked.

"Oh try walking through the vines. You don't know much do you? Are you a flower?"

"No, I am not a flower," Albert said.

"Ah you don't really look like one, but you never know with these sneaky flowers," the lizard said. Then he began muttering and looked suspiciously at a pumpkin flower nearby. He had forgotten about Albert. So, Albert walked over to the nearest vine. He looked and looked and looked for a way to get in. First he thought maybe he could make a wish, but there were no stars out. Then he got an idea.

"Abracadabra!" Albert said, waving his hand at the pumpkin vine.

Nothing happened.

"Open sesame!" he tried again.

Nothing happened.

"Please open!" he tried again.

Nothing happened.

"Oh I wish I were on the other side," Albert said, feeling sad again.

Suddenly there was a big whoosh and when Albert looked around he found himself in a tiny dark tunnel. He saw a light ahead and moved toward it. To keep from hitting his head he crawled. When he got to the light the tunnel widened. Albert was trying to be careful but it was slippery in the tunnel. Soon Albert found that he was sliding down the tunnel. It felt like a waterslide as the tunnel twisted and curved and even looped. Albert screamed in delight. Finally he landed on what felt like a soft, thick carpet.

Albert squinted but he couldn't see much. He decided to walk around when the room began to shake and Albert noticed that light was coming through the ceiling. More and more light was coming into the room, as the roof seemed to open. Eventually, the room was flooded with light and there was Albert's mother standing over him. He was in the belly of a pumpkin. Now he knew how water got into the belly of the pumpkin. He had even been there. Albert danced with delight.

"Albert. Wake up honey," his mother called. "It's time to get up."

Albert opened his eyes. He had been asleep the whole time. It had all been a dream. Then his mother looked at him as though she had never seen him before in her life.

"Albert," she said, "you're yellow. You're as yellow as the belly of a pumpkin." She grabbed him out of the bed and rushed him to the bathroom. She scrubbed him, and scrubbed him and scrubbed him again. When she was done Albert was squeaky clean, but he was still a lovely pumpkin yellow.

THE END

Primrose
The River & Mumma

One day Primrose was sent to the shop to buy groceries for her mother. On her way she had to cross a river. In the rainy season she would have to walk around the river because the heavy water would wash her away. During the dry season there were parts of the river where she could jump from stone to stone to get to the other side without getting her shoes wet. Primrose also knew to be careful of the part of the river called Monkey Hole where the water was always deep. Nobody that Primrose knew had ever found the bottom of Monkey Hole.

When Primrose came to the river, she stopped to play. Her mother had told her to hurry, but Primrose loved to make stones skip across the water. As she wandered up and down looking for the flat stones to throw, she noticed a beautiful comb lying on the river bank. Primrose had never seen anything so beautiful. She picked up the comb and it sparkled as the sun hit the jewels on the handle.

"Little girl," a voice said. Primrose looked up and there sitting on a rock was the most beautiful woman Primrose had ever seen. It was the River Mumma. She had long black hair, flawless brown skin and looked like she was made up completely of water. Primrose tried to speak but she could not. She could only think about how beautiful the woman was.

"Come little girl, come. Never mind what your mama tell you. Come little girl come," said the River Mumma and Primrose followed her. Soon the two of them were in the middle of the river moving toward Monkey Hole.

"Come little girl, come. Never mind what your mama tell you. Come little girl come," the woman said again, and Primrose continued to follow her. Primrose could feel the water rising past her ankles, then her knees and up past her waist. After a while they began to sink down, down, down, to the bottom of Monkey Hole.

When they reached the bottom of the river Primrose saw a beautiful palace. Like the woman, the palace seemed

to have been made from water, but you could not see through the walls. The woman stretched her hand out, touched the wall and sang:

> *River Mumma say you fi open. River Mumma want*
> *you fi open. River Mumma need you fi open. So wall*
> *you better open.*

The wall opened and the River Mumma pushed Primrose inside and the wall slammed shut behind them. The house was filled with other children. They were dusting, cleaning, mopping and sweeping. None of them said a word and they all looked very sad. There were little boys and big boys, little girls and big girls. Like Primrose, all of them had been caught by the River Mumma when they stopped to play at the river instead of going where their mother had sent them.

"You little girl, start dusting," said the River Mumma and dropped a huge cloth before Primrose. Primrose hated dusting. Sometimes when she had dusting to do at home she would hide and then pretend she had forgotten. When Primrose opened her mouth to protest, no sound came out.

"Children are to be seen and not heard," the woman said. "Now get to work," and with that she gave Primrose a push and walked away. Primrose wanted to yell at her, but she could not speak.

Primrose had never worked so hard in all her life. There was a lot of furniture to dust. Primrose did not

understand how dust got on furniture that was under the river, but it did. First was a huge dining room, with a very big table that had over 100 chairs. Then she had to go from bedroom to bedroom dusting all the furniture there. The rooms went on for three miles. There was one mile of green rooms, one mile of red rooms and one mile of yellow rooms. When Primrose finished the last room and stepped out into the hall the River Mumma was waiting outside. She silently indicated that Primrose should follow her. They got to a green wall and the woman pressed her palm to it and sang:

*River Mumma say you fi open. River Mumma want
you fi open. River Mumma need you fi open. So wall
you better open.*

The wall opened and Primrose was pushed inside. All the other children were inside and for the first time since Primrose had reached the River Mumma's palace she heard voices. Many of the children were crying loudly. Some stared ahead of them sadly. Primrose did not want to become like one of them. She pressed her hand to the wall and repeated the words the River Mumma sang:

*River Mumma say you fi open. River Mumma want
you fi open. River Mumma need you fi open. So wall
you better open.*

Nothing happened.

"It only works if you're a big person," one of the older boys said, but Primrose refused to give up. She tried and tried until her voice went hoarse. The next day when the woman came to put them to work, Primrose decided to watch her to see if there was any other way to escape, but she learnt nothing. Every night she tried the chant until she was hoarse, but the wall never opened until the next morning. Soon Primrose began to lose hope. She thought she would never see her mother again and it made her very sad.

One day, she decided that she would take no more. She would do no more pointless cleaning. That night when she went back to the room where the children stayed she told the others her plan.

"I'm going to strike," she said.

"What?" asked Courtney. He was a very jumpy boy and was more afraid of the River Mumma than anybody else.

"I'm not doing any more work," Primrose said.

"But-but-but the River Mumma will be mad? What if she beats us, or worse?" asked Courtney, his eyes wide with fright.

"I'm not afraid of her," lied Primrose.

"Yes you are," said Vanessa. "We're all afraid of her."

"Just because I'm afraid, doesn't mean I can't stand up to her. My mother says that

sometimes you have to stand up to your fears," said Primrose.

"Is true that," added Ricardo. He was a very quiet boy, and so when he spoke the other children tended to listen to him.

The children argued well into the night, and finally Primrose was able to convince them. The next morning when the River Mumma came to get them and put them to

work, nobody moved. Somehow all of them managed to be cowering behind Primrose so it was at her that the River Mumma pointed.

"Girl, what is going on?" the River Mumma asked loudly.

At first Primrose was so frightened she could not speak. Then she thought of her mother and how she must be worried about her.

"We're on strike," she told the River Mumma.

"Strike!" said the River Mumma. "You can't strike!"

"We strike!" said Primrose speaking louder. The River Mumma began to look very angry. Even her hair seemed angry. Then Primrose saw that the River Mumma looked very funny when she was mad. Her eyes widened and her nose flared. Before Primrose could help it, a tiny laugh came out. At the sound of her laughter the River Mumma covered her ears and screamed. Primrose had found her

weakness. The River Mumma hated the sound of children's laughter. So Primrose laughed and laughed and laughed and laughed. She turned all the tears she felt inside into laughter. She thought of everything funny she had ever heard and laughed even louder.

Soon the River Mumma was on the ground wriggling in pain. "Please stop," she begged Primrose. "I'll do anything if you stop."

"Will you let us go?" asked Primrose.

"Yes, I'll let you go. I'll let all of you go," the River Mumma said, tears streaming down her face.

"And promise never to steal any children from our village again?"

"Yes, yes," the River Mumma said. "Just don't laugh anymore."

On seeing that the River Mumma was weak and could not harm them anymore all the children ran out the door and out the palace. Then they swam up the river and ran home, their laughter filling the air.

The End

A GLASS HOUSE FOR BREDDA DOG

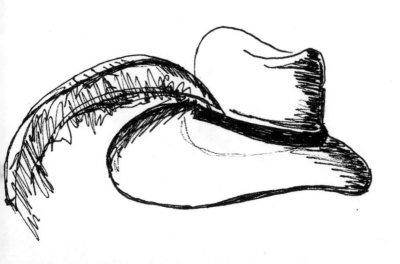

Once there was a time when dogs walked and talked just like people. All the animals used to. Some of them still do, but they talk in a language that people no longer understand. Bredda Dog used to live in those times. This is the story of how Bredda Dog was poor, got rich, and became poor again.

How did that happen? Well, like most people, once Bredda Dog got rich, he also lost much of his common sense. As the saying goes, when Bredda Dog has money, he'll buy cheese. Now if you've ever seen cheese and seen a dog's teeth you know the two don't mix. Dogs can't eat cheese.

For most of his life, Bredda Dog was poor and happy. He liked going to the river to fetch water everyday where he would play, catch some janga and either sun himself or lie in the shade. Bredda Dog liked cooking his food on a wood fire. His clothes were patched, but he liked the colours, and

thought of it as getting to wear many outfits at one time.

One day Bredda Dog met his old friend Bredda Puss whom he had not seen in a long time. Bredda Puss was wearing a lime green suit that he said brought out the colour of his huge green eyes. He had a shiny gold watch chain dangling across his belly and disappearing into his breast pocket. Bredda Puss also had on a lime green felt hat, with a large red feather stuck in the side, a red tie and red alligator skin shoes. Bredda Puss wore the hat so low on his forehead you could barely see his eyes.

"Where you been Bredda Puss?" Bredda Dog asked, excited to see his old friend.

"Been all over the world, Bredda Dog," Bredda Puss said. "I've been all over the world."

Poor Bredda Dog had only been to town once and all the busses and push carts and vendors had frightened him so badly he never returned. He was impressed that his schoolmate had travelled the world. Bredda Puss' clothes looked so fine next to Bredda Dog's that for the first time in his life Bredda Dog felt poor. Bredda Puss told Bredda Dog about houses made completely of glass and beds covered in jewels. Bredda Puss took the watch from his pocket, twirled it and it glistened in the sunlight. Bredda Dog believed Bredda Puss' story not knowing that Bredda Puss had never even gone as far as the other side of the island.

"Oh you should have seen them, Bredda Dog. The beds

were covered in jewels," said Bredda Puss ending his very tall tale. Then he turned to Bredda Dog and said, "You know with a little hard work one of those houses could be yours." Of course, Bredda Puss had never done a hard day's work in his life.

When Bredda Puss left, Bredda Dog looked at his own wooden house and imagined living in one of glass. Bredda Dog started to work much harder than he used to. Bredda Dog wanted a sheet studded with jewels and most of all he wanted a house made completely of glass. So Bredda Dog worked and

worked and worked some more. While he worked he saved and saved and saved some more. After a time Bredda Dog became rich, then richer and richer. He put all the money he saved under a mattress. When the mattress became too lumpy from the money stuck under it, Bredda Dog built a room for it. He kept the room locked so no one would rob him. But then nobody would think to rob Bredda Dog because he looked so poor a church mouse would give him money.

When the room was so full of money that Bredda Dog could barely squeeze himself into it, he decided he must have enough money. Bredda Dog climbed up to the top of the huge money pile and started to count. He counted and counted and counted for days, barely stopping to eat and drink. When he finished counting he went in search of Bredda Puss and found him sleeping under some mango trees.

"Bredda Puss," called Bredda Dog softly, not wanting to frighten Bredda Puss. Bredda Puss lifted his hat off his face and opened one eye.

"What do you need?" asked Bredda Puss, annoyed at having his second midday nap disturbed.

"Well I'm ready to make the house," said Bredda Dog.

"House?" asked Bredda Puss, lazily inspecting his claws. "What house?"

"A house of glass," said the excited Bredda Dog.

"What?" asked Bredda Puss. He had forgotten the tale he had told Bredda Dog. "You want a house made out of

39

pure glass? But that's crazy."

"But you told me about it Bredda Puss and I want one," said Bredda Dog.

"Oh yes, yes," said Bredda Puss finally catching on. He opened both eyes and looked at Bredda Dog, "You have money?" he asked.

"Yes man," said Bredda Dog. "I have a room full of money."

"Then I know some people who know some people who know some other people who can easily set you up," said Bredda Puss. So it was that Bredda Puss started to plan how he could get his paws on Bredda Dog's money. Bredda Puss put his arm around Bredda Dog and started leading him down the path. "Come Bredda Dog we have lots of talking to do."

The next day, a terrific noise woke up Bredda Dog. Bredda Puss was leading a group of people into the yard. Before Bredda Dog could reach outside they started to measure everything. They measured the space from the tamarind tree to the guinep tree. They even measured the trees themselves. They nodded and harrumphed, or grumbled or smiled. Bredda Dog rushed outside to find out what was happening.

"We're building your dream house man," Bredda Puss told him and Bredda Dog smiled a happy smile. Bredda Puss told Bredda Dog that in a very short time the house would be finished. The sly puss also told Bredda Dog to go and stay with his cousin in the next village so that the workmen could go faster. Bredda Puss tried to convince Bredda Dog to leave the key for the money room, but Bredda Dog said he would keep the key but would leave as much money as Bredda Puss needed. Bredda Dog didn't feel he could completely trust Bredda Puss. Well, if Bredda Dog had listened to his mind, this would be the story of how Bredda Dog got rich and stayed rich.

At the end of the week Bredda Dog came to look at the house. Bredda Dog's jaw dropped. The glass house glittered and shimmered. He could not believe his eyes.

"Do you like the house?" purred Bredda Puss coming up to him.

"Oh Bredda Puss, thank you! Thank you. Thank you. Thank you. Thank you. Thank you. Thank you. Thank you," said Bredda Dog his voice getting louder with each word. Bredda Dog was so grateful that when Bredda Puss asked him if it was okay for him to go into the money room and take a little bonus, Bredda Dog said yes, and gave Bredda Puss the key. Bredda Dog could not believe this shiny glass house was all his. When Bredda Dog got into the house he was even happier, even though he kept falling on the slippery glass floor. He finally made it to the bedroom and jumped on his bed that was covered in jewels.

"Ow! Ow! Ow! Ow! Ow! Ow!" screamed Bredda Dog as he hit against the jewels. Bredda Dog rubbed his injured side. He realized that having jewels on a bed was not a smart idea, as it wouldn't make for comfortable sleeping. He also started to think that maybe a house of glass was a bad idea. He had no privacy and he kept sliding on the floors. He realized he would have to build a real house with the money he had left.

As Bredda Dog considered this he looked closely at the jewels on the bed. He saw that they were not jewels. They were ordinary river stones and bits of glass painted to look shiny. Bredda Dog realized that he was tricked. When he looked through the glass wall, Bredda Dog saw Bredda Puss running from his yard with two very full bags of money. The door to the money room swung open. The room was empty.

Bredda Dog made a mad dash toward the door to try to stop Bredda Puss. But poor Bredda Dog, in his haste he slammed the glass door behind him. As he ran out into the yard he heard a crack. He stopped and turned to look back as the crack zigg-zagged its way in a million little lines all around the house. Then there was a loud crash and the house lay in a shiny heap on the ground. His house, his beautiful glass house was no more. He had no money and no house.

Bredda Dog searched and searched but could not find Bredda Puss. Since that day Bredda Puss and Bredda Dog have never been friends, and Bredda Dog knows not to waste money.

The End

The Guava Tree

**eisha was a young girl who lived in a** village high in the mountains. She lived with her stepfather, her mother having died when she was just a very little girl. Keisha's stepfather reared pigs, goats and cows. He also grew crops like red peas, corn, callaloo, cabbage, and pak choi.

Every morning before school, Keisha had to tie out the goats and feed the pigs and in the evening when she returned home from school she had to bring the goats back into their pen. When she came back with the goats she then had to prepare dinner and wash her stepfather's clothes.

Her stepfather treated her very badly. When her mother was alive he treated her well, but once her mother died he became mean. He worked Keisha very hard and gave her very little to eat and so she was a very skinny girl.

One day when Keisha took the goats out into the field, the Billy goat was being very stubborn and tried to drag her about. Because the goat was very strong it ended up pulling Keisha to a part of the field that nobody went to anymore. The place was overgrown with weeds.

In the middle to the tall winter grass was a large guava tree with lovely ripe guavas on it. Keisha was so hungry. She quickly picked some of the

fruit and started to eat. It was the most delicious thing she had ever eaten. The first fruit tasted just like a guava, but when she picked the next fruit it tasted like brown stewed chicken, another fruit tasted like roasted yellow yam and yet another tasted like ackee and salt fish.

Keisha was so happy, she wanted to go on eating forever but she knew she

should not be too greedy because she would need to come to the tree again. That night when Keisha got home she was happier than she remembered being for a very long time. She went to bed happy, not minding the cold winds that came across the mountain and made its way under the thin covers. While she slept she dreamt. She dreamt of her mother sitting below the guava tree.

"Keisha my girl; my one and only child," said her mother stroking Keisha's head, "I planted this tree right here so for you. Don't worry, I plant your navel string under that tree, and for as long as you live, it will grow. I did that because I wanted to make sure that you would get everything you deserve. The tree will take care of you," and with that she was gone.

Keisha wanted to tell her mother how much she loved her. She felt good knowing that her mother had planted a tree for her and so would take care of her. For the first time in a long time Keisha woke up happy.

Keisha returned to the tree every day. In the morning when she came to tie out the goats she ate breakfast from it. She put a few guavas in her pocket for lunch and in the evening when she came to take the goats

back home she ate dinner. Keisha was careful to still eat what her stepfather gave her. She did not want to make him suspicious. She knew that if she stopped eating the crust of bread and butter that he gave her for breakfast or the little food he gave her in the evening he would realize that she

was getting food from somewhere else.

Though Keisha tried to make everything appear normal, after a while her stepfather noticed that she was getting fatter. She no longer looked like skin and bones and her skin now glowed a healthy brown. So one day he decided to follow her to see where she was getting food. Her stepfather was sure that she was stealing from him. He followed her to their field, saw her tie out the goats and then go down into her mother's old garden. While he lay on his belly in the tall grass he watched as she picked the fruit and ate them.

The stepfather could not believe his eyes. How could she be getting fat on guavas? The fruits must be made of magic he thought. So after Keisha left he decided to try to pick some of the fruits. He realized that if they were magic guavas he would make a fortune at the market. The stepfather reached up to the nearest fruit but he could not pick it. It was just out of his reach. He was sure that it had been lower. So he tried to jump and pick it, but still he could not reach it. He tried to climb the tree but the trunk just kept getting taller and taller. He could not reach the fruits. Finally in anger he went for his cutlass and chopped the tree down.

The stepfather then waited in the bushes to see what would happen when Keisha came back in the evening. When the young girl came and found the tree lying on the ground with the fruits already starting to whither, she burst into tears.

"Oh my mother, you see how they are treating your one pickney, your only child. What am I to do now mother? How do I get what I deserve when the tree that you left me is gone?" And she cried until night came and then took home her goats. But that night she was so sad, she did not even eat her crust of bread.

After Keisha wandered home, her stepfather got an idea. He took up one of the guavas from the ground and carried it home. When he got there he planted it in his own special garden just above the house. He hoped that like Keisha, he would get what he deserved. The next morning when he awoke, Keisha's stepfather went to look at the plant. Overnight it had grown into a massive tree, but the fruits on it were not guavas. They were long whip-like things. It was a mama-lashee tree. As far as the stepfather knew the fruit could not be eaten but he thought maybe this one was different. Keisha's stepfather reached toward the tree, but as he did the whip-like fruits began to flail and he had to duck to keep from being hit. As he cowered at the foot of the tree, the tree showed him images of how Keisha had suffered and how he had treated her badly because he was so consumed by despair when her mother had died.

The stepfather felt great regret over his behaviour. He knew that he had treated his stepdaughter badly and wanted

to make it up to her but he did not know how.

In the mean time, Keisha had taken the goats to the field. She had already mourned the loss of her tree but she was not a fenke-fenke girl. Even when she was quite skinny, the years spent carrying a bucket of water on her head, or cutting and carrying home wood for the fire had made her quite strong. She was also a good farmer. So she went to see if the tree had completely died. When she got to the spot, she realized that there was a chance to save the bit of trunk that was left. Keisha began to tend the tree and try to coax it back to life.

When she got home that night, she found her stepfather in bed, he was very sick having been overcome by grief. He apologized to her for the way he had treated her over the years.

"Keisha I beg you to forgive me," he said. "I did not realize what I was doing to you. I am so sorry. Your poor mother left you in my care and look how I treated you?"

Though Keisha felt a lot of resentment in her heart, she knew better than to keep bitterness inside because that only made you unhappy. So she forgave her stepfather. Not long after, he died. With the help of the villagers who took pity on the young orphan girl, Keisha grew to be a great farmer and was renowned for making the best guava jam in the country.

The End

The Thing With The Tale

Retold

Once upon a time, it could be any time at all even today, in a country very much like this one there lived a boy named Berry. Now his real name wasn't Berry. Berry was just what everyone called him because he loved cheese berries. Cheese berries used to grow all over the mountainside. They were tiny yellow fruits, more the colour of sunshine than cheese. Cheese berries grow on skinny shrubs, covered in tiny brown makka that would often prick you when you reached for a delicious berry.

Berry was not skilled at avoiding the pricks from the makka. All he cared about was getting to his beloved berries. He would worry about the pain from the thorns later. The cheese berries were plentiful where Berry lived. When he was younger he used to sit in the yard and eat all the berries his mother brought him. Berry would eat and eat and eat and eat, until even his shirt had gone yellow with the stains from the fruit. When the last berry was gone he would lick the juice from his fingers not wanting any to go to waste.

Berry and his mother lived in a tiny wooden house at the edge of the Bush. When he was much younger, his father used to live with them, but one day his father left for work in the woods and never came back. Berry had waited and waited for his father to come back, pressing his face to the window. But his father did not come. Berry closed his eyes and wished with all his might. But his father did not come. He asked his mother where papa was.

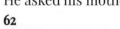

"Yuh fadda gawn a Bush," his mother said, and he could never get her to say why he was taking so long to come back.

As Berry grew older his mother began to leave him alone in the house while she went out to work in the Bush. Berry's mother was a wise woman. She knew the dangers lurking in the Bush where she worked and why his father had not returned. He had been bewitched. She made sure to tell Berry to be careful while she was gone. She would prefer to stay home with him, but she had to go out to work and bring home food for them.

Every morning before she left, Berry's mother said to him, "Berry don't let anybody at all into the house."

And he would answer, "Yes mama."

"Who I say you must let in?" she asked.

"Nobody mama," Berry answered.

"An if dem say dem come to me?" she asked.

"Don't let them in," Berry replied.

"An if dey say I send dem to you?" she asked again.

"Don't let them in," Berry replied obediently.

This went on for a long time. Every morning when Berry's mother was ready to leave the house she would ask him the same questions and he would give her the same answers.

Then one day, just like any other day, when the sun was a bright yellow ball in the sky covering the world with warmth, Berry's mother changed the ritual just a little bit. It started in the same way.

"Berry don't let anybody at all into the house."

And he answered, "Yes mama."

"Who I say you must let in?" she asked.

"Nobody mama," Berry replied.

"An if dem say dem come to me?" she asked.

"Don't let them in," Berry replied.

"An if deh say I send dem to you?" she asked again.

"Don't let them in," Berry replied obediently. His mother was almost through the door when she turned back to him and asked.

"Berry, you don't go and play in the Bush when I not here?"

"No mama," he denied quickly, surprised by her question.

Berry had thought about going into the Bush especially to pick berries, but so far there were enough to satisfy him in the yard.

"Make sure you don't go and play in the forest," she said. She gripped his chin and tilted his head up so she was looking into her eyes when she spoke. "Stay in the yard."

"Yes mama," he promised.

This went on for quite some time, and Berry stayed in the yard while his mother was away. Then one day he began to wonder what was out in the Bush. He could not imagine anything really dangerous out there. After all, his mother went there every day. True, she was a tall, strong woman, but he did not think she could handle a monster. Little by little, Berry began to be less afraid of nameless monsters in the Bush. The berries on the bushes in the yard were getting fewer everyday and Berry thought about all the delicious berries he could find in the Bush just waiting to be picked. Berry could almost taste the ripe, juicy, yellow berries he would find. As he thought about them, his mouth began to water.

One day, Berry decided to go just a little way into the Bush to find berries. He told himself that his mother had said he shouldn't go to play in the forest, not that he couldn't go there to pick berries. He had not gone far when he found a bush loaded with the golden treasure. A look of sheer delight came over Berry and his dark brown eyes danced with joy. Not bothering to put any in the bag he had brought, Berry started to eat right there. Berry was so happy he did not pay attention to the makka as it scratched his skin. He ate and ate and ate and ate and ate until he thought he would burst. Only then did Berry stop and start to feel the stinging from the tiny cuts on his skin. Bruised but happy, Berry made his way back home. He had not gone far so he was soon home.

Berry continued to go back to that cheese berry bush.

When there were no more berries left on that bush he went a little farther into the forest. He finished the next bush and then went a little farther. Day by day, Berry went a little farther, and a little farther, and a little farther into the woods. Finally one day, Berry found himself deep in the Bush. For the first time, Berry realized how tall the trees around him were. There were towering white-barked eucalyptus trees, pines trees and tree ferns.

When Berry looked up he felt very, very, very, very small. He felt a tingling at the back of his neck as though someone was watching him. Berry looked around quickly. He saw nothing but trees. He looked to the left and he looked to the right, but there were only more trees. Berry was afraid. He could feel the fear spreading from his feet, to his hands and up to his head, and that fear told his feet to run.

Forgetting the juicy berries still on the bush, Berry took his feet in his hands and ran as fast as he could. He ran, and ran, and ran until he got home. He ran into the house and locked the door behind him, panting for breath. He promised himself he would never go into the Bush again.

The next day, after his mother left, Berry did not even want to go out into the yard. Ignoring the bright sunlight streaming through the curtains and inviting him to come out and play, he stayed inside. At lunchtime, he went to dish out his turn cornmeal. His mother made the best turn cornmeal with vegetables, peas and chunks of chicken. Berry loved the chunks of chicken. Next to berries, he loved chicken best. Berry was about to start eating when there was a knock at the door.

Berry froze. No one had ever come to the door when he was at home alone before.

"Who is it?" Berry squeaked. No answer came.

Berry crept up to the window to see outside. He didn't see any one. Had he imagined the knock? Before he could relax, the knock came again. Louder.

"G'wey!" Barry squeaked, trying to be brave. "My madda say mi not to let in nobody."

Again no answer.

Soon another knock came, louder still. Frightened but trying to be brave, Berry ran to the door and pulled it open, planning to tell the rude person to go away.

"Mi say fi –" the words died on his lips as he saw the thing standing at the door. It was short and skinny, so skinny you could see the bones beneath its skin. It almost looked like a man but it had a long bushy tail. Worst of all, it was smiling at him, revealing jagged sharp teeth. In fear, Berry stepped back from the doorway and The Thing walked right into the house.

"Where yuh mumma deh?" it demanded in a deep scratchy voice.

"She gaawn a bush," Berry answered, so scared he could barely speak.

"Where yuh puppa deh?" The Thing asked.

Berry didn't really know where his father was, but the Thing looked like it would eat him, if he didn't answer. So he gave him the answer his mother had given him when his father first disappeared.

"Him – him gaawn a bush," Berry said.

"Where yuh lunch deh?" The thing demanded.

"It deh pon the table," Berry answered, so frightened his teeth were beginning to clatter. The Thing went over to the table and ate up all of Berry's lunch, not leaving a single deggeh-deggeh crumb. When it had finished it turned around in a circle and lay in front of the table.

"Play wid me tail make me sleep," it said. Not knowing what else to do, Berry did as he was told. He had not meant to let the thing in, but now it was in and it had eaten all his lunch. Berry wanted to cry, but he was afraid of waking the thing. It had fallen asleep as soon as Berry began playing with its tail. Berry didn't know when it happened, but he too must have fallen asleep. He awoke to the sound of his mother coming home. As soon as he was fully awake he remembered the thing, but he saw no sign of it. He decided it must have been a dream.

The next day, Berry's mother gave him the usual instructions before she left. This time when Berry promised not to let anyone in, he meant it. He remembered his dream clearly. Berry did not feel like going out to look for berries. Thinking of going outside made him feel all funny in his belly. So, he stayed inside instead and played marbles by himself. By lunchtime Berry was starving.

He was getting up to eat when there was a knock at the door. Without thinking, and forgetting everything his mother had told him about not letting anybody into the house, Berry opened the door. As soon as he did, he realized his mistake. The Thing walked right into the house, as if he owned it.

"Where yuh mumma deh?" it demanded.

"She gaawn a bush," Berry answered.

"Where yuh puppa deh?" The Thing asked.

"Him gaawn a bush." Berry answered, his voice trembling.

"Where yuh lunch deh?" came the deep scratchy voice.

"It deh pon the table," Berry said. The Thing went over to the table and ate up all of Berry's lunch, once again without leaving a single deggeh-deggeh crumb. When it finished it turned around in a circle and lay in front of the table.

"Play with me tail make me sleep," it said. Once again Berry obeyed and as soon as he started to play with the bushy tail, The Thing fell asleep. Berry was very sorry he had not listened to his mother. He was sorry he had gone to look for berries. He was sorry he had let the thing in although his mother told him everyday not to let anyone in. He just wanted his mother.

Berry's mother had thought something was wrong when she got home the day before because Berry seemed much hungrier than usual, as if he had not eaten his lunch. She was beginning to think that maybe he was sick. Then, when she was cleaning the house that morning, she saw some long red hairs on the carpet. She knew what that meant.

So, she crept home to see what happened in the house while she was at work. When she looked through the window Berry's mother saw a sobbing Berry playing with the tail of the sleeping Thing. She knew what it was. It was a creature

called the maw-ma man. It used to be a real man, but now it would just feed off little children and their mothers. Once one began coming to your house it would never go away.

Berry's mother took out the cutlass she used in the woods all day and burst through the door. The maw-ma man jumped up and Berry's mother swiftly cut its head off. Without a sound it fell down dead.

When it hit the ground, its body began to stretch and widen. Soon it no longer looked like an animal, but a real

73

man. As the man stood up the red hair fell to the ground to reveal dark brown skin. Berry could not believe what he was seeing. He knew this man.

"Papa?" Berry said in a small voice. When the man smiled at him, Berry gave a shout of joy. He could not believe that his father was home. Berry wrapped his arms around his father's legs. The big man picked him up with one arm, and then used the other to hold Berry's mother close. Berry had never been so happy in his life.

Berry's father took him on his lap and told him, about how he had been bewitched and turned into the Thing that came to terrorize poor Berry. He had been drawn to the house when Berry came looking for the cheese berries. Berry promised never to go out into the forest alone again, and he never did.

Not even for cheese berries.

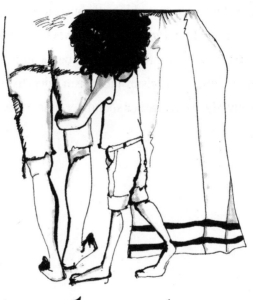

The End

Tanya Batson-Savage

Tanya Batson-Savage loves mangoes and stories, and stories about mangoes. She has written for the stage, screen and radio (and one day will write a story about a mango). Her love of stories grew while she was seated at her grandmother's feet where she developed a love of folk tales that shines through in her first collection of stories for children *'Pumpkin Belly and Other Stories'*. Her career has crisscrossed the cultural landscape including cultural policy, teaching, cultural criticism, journalism, advertising, and publicity. But really, she would rather spend her time eating mangoes.

Staysean Daley

Staysean is a visual communicator at her very core. She was born in Venezuela to Jamaican parents. An illustrator and designer, Staysean was raised in Jamaica with an infusion of arts and culture the love of which permeates every fibre of her being. Staysean's formal training in Visual Arts began at the Edna Manley College of the Visual Arts in Kingston, Jamaica and was completed at the Miami International University of Art and Design with a BFA in Graphic Design. With several years in advertising under her belt, she is the founder and CEO of Kraas Images producers of authentic Caribbean stock photography.

You can learn more about her work at:
kraasdesigns.com
kraasimages.com

Irie Morning

By Alison Moss-Solomon &
illustrated by Adom Burke

SOMETIMES GETTING UP IS HARD TO DO!

Kingston has a problem. He doesn't want to get up. The sun is shining, the birds by the seaside are calling and even the dogs are asking him to come out and play, but Kingston would rather sleep the day away.

Will he let the day pass him by? Or will he discover that there is always a lot to do on an Irie Morning

Perfect for 0–5 year-olds

Bolo the Monkey

By Jonathan Burke &
illustrated by Nicholas Martin

ONE DARING MONKEY AND A DREAM

Bolo the Monkey was daring to be bold, But monkeys don't farm he was told! They don't spend all day digging a hole. A monkey is a monkey, not a squirrel or a mole!

This is the story of one daring little monkey who tries to change his world, as all little monkeys should.

Perfect for 0-8 year-olds

All Over Again

By A-dZiko Simba Gegele

Who knew growing up could be so hard.

Growing up is hard. You know this. And when your mother has X-ray eyes and dances like a wobbling bag of water? When Kenny, Percival Thorton High's big show-off, is after Christina Parker - your Christina Parker? And when you have a shrimp of a little sister who is the bawlingest little six year old girl in the whole of Riverland? Then growing up is something you not sure you can manage at all. Who in their right mind could? Who? You?

All Over Again is an enchanting slice of boyhood. It is a charming coming of age story with a bold narrative style that pulls you into it.

Winner of the 2014 Burt Award for Caribbean Literature and longlisted for the 2015 International IMPAC Dublin Literary Award